FEB 2022

MW01129714

Lerner SPORTS

SPORTS' GREATEST OF ALL TIME

GYMNASTICS'S
G.O.A.T.

NADIA COMANECI, SIMONE BILES, AND MORE

JOE LEVIT

Lerner Publications ◆ Minneapolis

LAKE VILLA DISTRICT LIBRARY
847.356.7711 www.lvdl.org

SCORE BIG with sports fans, reluctant readers, and report writers!

Lerner Sports is a database of high-interest biographies profiling notable sports superstars. Packed with fascinating facts, these bios explore the backgrounds, career-defining moments, and everyday lives of popular athletes. Lerner Sports is perfect for young readers developing research skills or looking for exciting sports content.

LERNER SPORTS FEATURES:

- ✔ Keyword search
- ✔ Topic navigation menus
- ✔ Fast facts
- ✔ Related bio suggestions to encourage more reading
- ✔ Admin view of reader statistics
- ✔ Fresh content updated regularly

and more!

Visit LernerSports.com **for a free trial!**

Lerner SPORTS

Copyright © 2022 by Lerner Publishing Group, Inc.

All rights reserved. International copyright secured. No part of this book may be reproduced, stored in a retrieval system, or transmitted in any form or by any means—electronic, mechanical, photocopying, recording, or otherwise—without the prior written permission of Lerner Publishing Group, Inc., except for the inclusion of brief quotations in an acknowledged review.

Lerner Publications Company
An imprint of Lerner Publishing Group, Inc.
241 First Avenue North
Minneapolis, MN 55401 USA

For reading levels and more information, look up this title at www.lernerbooks.com.

Main body text set in Aptifer Sans LT Pro. Typeface provided by Linotype AG.

Editor: Rebecca Higgins **Designer:** Kim Morales

Library of Congress Cataloging-in-Publication Data

Names: Levit, Joseph, author.
Title: Gymnastics's G.O.A.T : Nadia Comaneci, Simone Biles, and more / Joe Levit.
Other titles: Gymnastic's greatest of all time
Description: Minneapolis : Lerner Publications, [2022] | Series: Sports' greatest of all time (Lerner sports) | Includes bibliographical references and index. | Audience: Ages 7–11 | Audience: Grades 4–6 | Summary: "From daring vaults to jaw-dropping floor routines, gymnastics stars do it all. This book sticks the landing for old and new fans alike with stunning stats, thrilling comebacks, and the greatest gymnasts of all time"— Provided by publisher.
Identifiers: LCCN 2021000079 (print) | LCCN 2021000080 (ebook) | ISBN 9781728428604 (library binding) | ISBN 9781728431581 (paperback) | ISBN 9781728430805 (ebook)
Subjects: LCSH: Gymnasts—Juvenile literature. | Gymnastics—Juvenile literature. | Comăneci, Nadia, 1961—-Juvenile literature. | Biles, Simone, 1997-—Juvenile literature.
Classification: LCC GV461.3 .L48 2022 (print) | LCC GV461.3 (ebook) | DDC 796.44092/2 [B]—dc23

LC record available at https://lccn.loc.gov/2021000079
LC ebook record available at https://lccn.loc.gov/2021000080

Manufactured in the United States of America
1-49397-49498-3/24/2021

TABLE OF CONTENTS

Gymnastics requires strength. Athletes can't complete skills without it.

STICK THE LANDING!

Great gymnasts have competed against one another for years in the Olympic Games and World Championships. Yet choosing which athlete is the greatest of all time (G.O.A.T.) is not a simple task.

FACTS AT A GLANCE

SVETLANA KHORKINA claimed the gold medal on the uneven bars at the 1995 and 2003 World Championships.

SAWAO KATO helped his team win the all-around title by 0.4 of a point.

NADIA COMANECI earned seven perfect scores at the 1976 Olympics.

SIMONE BILES has four elements named after her, including a floor exercise move that has the highest difficulty rating in women's gymnastics.

That's partly because scores changed after the 2004 Summer Olympics in Athens, Greece. Before those Games, a 10 was a perfect score. The new system is based on two different scores. One score rates the difficulty of a routine. The other score rates how well the gymnast performs. Before 1991, World Championships were held every four years. Since then, the events have taken place every two years, except for Olympic years. So modern gymnasts have more chances to earn medals.

Both men and women do floor and vault routines. And they both compete for team and individual all-around medals. But they also have different events. Women compete on the uneven bars and the balance beam. Men perform on the pommel horse, the rings, the parallel bars, and the horizontal bar.

The best gymnasts of all time have a few things in common. They have usually won an all-around gold medal in the Olympics. They are in the International Gymnastics Hall of Fame or are headed there. They have more medals than most other gymnasts have. And they often have gymnastics moves named after them.

Athletes have been raising the bar on the balance beam since it became part of the Olympics in 1952.

Gymnasts perform tough moves on the rings while trying to keep them still.

You may not be familiar with some of the names in this book. But it's impossible to tell the history of gymnastics without them. You might disagree with the rankings. Or you may feel that someone important has been left out. Your friends will have their own G.O.A.T. opinions. Disagreeing is part of the fun. Forming your own opinions about some of the world's top gymnasts is what this book is all about.

#10

SVETLANA KHORKINA

Svetlana Khorkina was a tall, graceful gymnast. But her height and long legs often made practicing gymnastics difficult, since flips and other exercises require more effort for taller gymnasts. She was forced to be creative with her routines. Khorkina created eight elements that are named after her: two types of vaults, two moves on the balance beam, one floor exercise jump, and three moves on the uneven bars.

In recent years, the group that oversees international gymnastics changed the ways it gives credit for elements. The changes meant Khorkina has only four named moves. Each shows how her originality produced something new and exciting. Her unique style was most on display on the uneven bars. She won the event at the World Championship in 2003, eight years after winning it for the first time.

SVETLANA KHORKINA STATS

- She won seven Olympic medals, two of them gold.

- She has 20 World Championship medals, nine of them gold.

- She was the first gymnast to earn three all-around World Championship titles.

- She won 20 European Women's Championship medals, 13 of them gold.

- She won two gold medals at the Goodwill Games in 1994.

OLGA KORBUT

When Olga Korbut performed, people noticed. Her fun style and winning grin earned her fans around the world. Her amazing skills convinced many to leap into the sport. At 14, Korbut competed in her first championship in the Soviet Union, a former country that included Russia. She finished fifth. But Korbut became the first gymnast

to complete two new moves in that event. One was a backward somersault on the balance beam. The other was a backward release and catch on the uneven bars. These moves became known as the Korbut salto and the Korbut flip.

Korbut thrilled spectators at the 1972 Olympics. The 17-year-old won gold medals in the balance beam and floor exercise. She was also part of the gold-winning Soviet team. She added a silver medal in the uneven bars. Her small size and grace earned her the nickname the Sparrow from Minsk. She won two more medals at the 1976 Olympics.

OLGA KORBUT STATS

- She won six Olympic medals, four of them gold.

- She won six medals, two of them gold, during her only World Championship.

- She won a silver all-around medal in the 1973 European Championships.

- She won the Russian and World Student Games in 1973.

- In 1988, she became the first athlete to join the International Gymnastics Hall of Fame.

NIKOLAI ANDRIANOV

Nikolai Andrianov began his gymnastics training at 12. That's a late start for a gymnast. But he made up for lost time. With a powerful body and great leaping ability, he became one of the sport's most accomplished athletes. An aggressive floor routine in the 1972 Olympics earned him a gold medal. He was at peak form four years later in the 1976 Olympics. He won seven medals, including four gold.

Andrianov was well known for doing difficult routines. His skill earned him two more gold medals in the 1980 Olympics. Andrianov finished his career with 15 Olympic medals. That ranks third in Olympic history. Gymnast Larisa Latynina is in second place with 18 medals. At the top is swimmer Michael Phelps with 28 medals.

NIKOLAI ANDRIANOV STATS

▶ He won seven Olympic gold medals.

▶ He won all-around gold at the 1976 Olympics.

▶ He won 13 World Championship medals, four of them gold.

▶ He won 17 European Championship medals, nine of them gold.

▶ He joined the International Gymnastics Hall of Fame in 2001.

#7

SAWAO KATO

Fans admired Sawao Kato for his original moves and precise movements. But his ability to perform under extreme pressure made him a winner. He led his fellow Japanese gymnasts against strong competition throughout his career. Kato and his teammates almost always came out on top.

Kato won the all-around gold medal at the 1968 Olympics. His teammates won three of the other four top places. Four years later, Kato again won the all-around gold. Japanese men took the gold, silver, and bronze all-around medals at that Olympics—the first clean sweep for one country in the men's Olympic all-around since 1900.

In 1976, Kato lost the individual all-around gold medal by a single point to Soviet gymnast Nikolai Andrianov. But Japan bested the Soviets for the third time in the team all-around. They won by 0.4 of a point!

SAWAO KATO STATS

▸ He won 12 Olympic medals.

▸ His eight Olympic gold medals are more than any other male gymnast has.

▸ He won all-around gold at both the 1968 and 1972 Olympics.

▸ He won all-around silver at the 1976 Olympics.

▸ He joined the International Gymnastics Hall of Fame in 2001.

#6

LARISA LATYNINA

Larisa Latynina entered her first Olympics at 21. Determined to succeed, she never backed down from a challenge. She even competed in the 1958 World Championship while four months pregnant! Her desire to succeed earned her a record 18 Olympic medals. No one could beat that for 48 years. Michael Phelps passed her overall total in 2012. But Latynina still holds the record for most individual medals won, with 14.

Latynina helped the Soviet Union win team gold in the 1956 and 1960 Olympics. She also won individual all-around titles in both of those Olympics. In 1964, she settled for silver in the individual all-around. But once more she led her country to a team gold medal.

LARISA LATYNINA STATS

- ▶ She won 18 Olympic medals overall, nine of them gold.

- ▶ She won six medals in each of three straight Olympics.

- ▶ She won all-around gold at both the 1956 and 1960 Olympics.

- ▶ She won 14 World Championship medals, nine of them gold.

- ▶ She joined the International Gymnastics Hall of Fame in 1998.

System Reuther

VERA CASLAVSKA

Vera Caslavska showed that standing up for what's right is more important than winning. Caslavska was a brilliant gymnast from Czechoslovakia. But she was also a political activist. Soviet military forces invaded Czechoslovakia in 1968 before the Olympic Games. Caslavska spoke out about these actions. She went into hiding because she feared she would be arrested. Caslavska kept up her

gymnastics training by using a log as a balance beam. She practiced floor exercises in a meadow.

Three weeks later, Caslavska rejoined her team for the Olympics and won the all-around gold. Four years before, Caslavska had won the same honor. She won gold in each of the individual events in the 1964 Olympics. She remains the only gymnast to have pulled off that feat.

VERA CASLAVSKA STATS

- She won 11 Olympic medals, seven of them gold.

- She won the all-around gold medal at both the 1964 and 1968 Olympics.

- She won 10 World Championship medals, four of them gold.

- She won 14 European Championship medals, 11 of them gold.

- She joined the International Gymnastics Hall of Fame in 1998.

VITALY SCHERBO

Athletes often use a major disappointment to ignite their greatest achievements. Vitaly Scherbo certainly did. He won the silver all-around medal at the 1991 World Championships. But that wasn't nearly good enough for Scherbo. He was determined to prove what he could do. A year later, he was golden.

Scherbo dominated at the 1992 Olympics. His peak performance is perhaps the single greatest gymnastics showing of all time. Scherbo won the team and all-around gold medals. Two days later, he finished first in the parallel bars, vault, and rings. Finally, he tied for first in the pommel horse. That made Scherbo the first person in Olympic history to win four gold medals in one day. He is also the only gymnast to earn six gold medals in a single Olympic competition.

VITALY SCHERBO STATS

▶ He won 10 Olympic medals, six of them gold.

▶ His 23 World Championship medals, 12 of them gold, trails only Simone Biles.

▶ He won the all-around gold medal in the 1992 Olympics.

▶ He won at least one world title in each event, and he has a vault named after him.

▶ He joined the International Gymnastics Hall of Fame in 2009.

#3

NADIA COMANECI

Nadia Comaneci brought worldwide attention to gymnastics during the 1976 Olympics. Her routine on the uneven bars earned her the first perfect 10.0 score in modern history. Scoreboards couldn't even show that result. Her score appeared as a 1.00 instead. It was a big moment for Comaneci and for fans in attendance and around the world. Comaneci went on to score six more

perfect 10s at that Olympics. She also earned the all-around gold medal, capping off her historic performance.

Comaneci was a success at the 1980 Olympics as well. She was always trying new moves. She has two named elements in the Code of Points, a rule book that explains the scoring system. Comaneci earned the Olympic Order award in 1984, the highest award given by the International Olympic Committee. Very few athletes ever receive the award. She is the only athlete to have won it twice.

NADIA COMANECI STATS

- She won nine Olympic medals, five of them gold.

- She won the all-around gold medal at the 1976 Olympics.

- She won four World Championship medals, two of them gold.

- She won 12 European Championship medals, nine of them gold.

- She joined the International Gymnastics Hall of Fame in 1993.

#2

KOHEI UCHIMURA

Kohei Uchimura is the definition of excellence. He won every major all-around title from 2009 to 2016. The streak included two Olympic golds and six World Championship titles. Before the streak, Uchimura earned all-around silver at the 2008 Olympics. That's nearly a decade of dominance. Many people consider him to be the greatest gymnast of all time. Nadia Comaneci agrees. She was

amazed by his eight-year undefeated streak. And she felt his skills were flawless.

Uchimura didn't just excel alone. He helped Japan land all-around team silver in the 2008 and 2012 Olympics. Four years later, Uchimura made sure that Japan got their gold medals. King Kohei's squad finished first at the 2016 Olympics.

KOHEI UCHIMURA STATS

▶ He has won seven Olympic medals, three of them gold.

▶ He has won 21 World Championship medals, 10 of them gold.

▶ He won the all-around gold medal at both the 2012 and 2016 Olympics.

▶ He won six World Championship all-around gold medals in a row.

▶ He plans to compete in the next Summer Olympics to try to add to his medal count.

London 2012

#1

SIMONE BILES

Many people believe that Simone Biles may already be the greatest gymnast in history. And yet she's still competing for more medals. Her stunning strength and amazing skills helped her rise to the top. Biles won five gold medals at the 2019 World Championship. That boosted her career total to 25. She jumped past Vitaly Scherbo in the record books. Scherbo's 23 World Championship medals hadn't been beaten in 23 years!

Biles makes difficult moves look easy. Her amazing skills allow her to try new things. She has four elements named after her. One is a floor exercise move that has the highest difficulty rating in all of women's gymnastics. It is a triple-twisting double-tucked backwards somersault. No other woman has landed the move. Gymnastics fans can't wait to see what Biles does next.

SIMONE BILES STATS

- She has won five Olympic medals, four of them gold.

- She has won 25 World Championship medals, 19 of them gold.

- She won the all-around gold medal at the 2016 Olympics.

- She has four named elements.

- She plans to compete in the next Summer Olympics in the all-around.

YOUR G.O.A.T.

IT'S YOUR TURN TO MAKE A G.O.A.T. LIST ABOUT TOP GYMNASTS. Score a perfect 10 by starting out with some research. Carefully consider the rankings in this book. Then check out the Learn More section on page 31. There you'll see books and websites that will give you more information about the top gymnasts of the past and present. Talk to your librarian to find other resources. You could even reach out to some current gymnasts to get their thoughts about who's on top.

Once you're ready, make your list of the greatest gymnasts of all time. Then ask your friends to make their own lists and compare them. Do you have gymnasts that no one else listed? Is the order of athletes similar or extremely different? Talk it over, and try to convince them that your list is the G.O.A.T.!

GYMNASTICS FACTS

► Simone Biles, at 4 feet 8 (1.4 m), can jump to 9 feet, 4 inches (2.8 m) during her floor exercises!

► The first perfect 10 in gymnastics occurred in 1924, when 23 men earned the score in rope climbing. The event was soon dropped from the Olympics.

► In gymnastics, 44 women have earned medals for the United States. The Soviet Union is second with 42.

► Kerri Strug vaulted with an injured ankle at the 1996 Olympics and helped her team win a gold medal.

GLOSSARY

all-around: when an athlete competes in all of the events and is given a score in each event

balance beam: gymnastics equipment with a 4-inch-wide (10 cm) beam

Code of Points: a rule book with the scoring system and approved moves for gymnastics competitions

element: a gymnastics move in a routine

horizontal bar: gymnastics equipment with one high bar

pommel horse: gymnastics equipment with a rectangular body and two hand grips, or pommels

rings: gymnastics equipment consisting of two rings attached to cords high in the air

routine: the series of elements and artistic moves that gymnasts perform

salto: a somersault

uneven bars: gymnastics equipment with two bars at different heights

LEARN MORE

Blackaby, Susan. *Simone Biles: Making the Case for the Greatest of All Time.* New York: Sterling Children's Books, 2019.

International Gymnastics Federation
http://www.gymnastics.sport/site/

International Gymnastics Hall of Fame
https://www.ighof.com/

Lawrence, Blythe. *Behind the Scenes Gymnastics.* Lerner Publications, 2020.

Lawrence, Blythe. *Best Male Gymnasts of All Time.* Minneapolis: Abdo, 2020.

USA Gymnastics
https://usagym.org/

INDEX

PHOTO ACKNOWLEDGMENTS

Image credits: backgrounds: Eugene Onischenko/Shutterstock.com; CasarsaGuru/ Getty Images, p. 4; ssj414/E+/Getty Images, p. 6; bilderlounge/Tips RF/Getty Images, p. 7; AP Photo/SUE OGROCK, p. 8; AP Photo/Breloer Gero, p. 9 (all); AP Photo, pp. 10, 11 (bottom), 15 (all), 16, 22, 23 (all); AP Photo/SUZANNE VLAMIS, p. 11 (top); Leo Mason/Popperfoto/Getty Images, p. 12; SPUTNIK/Alamy Stock Photo, p. 13 (top); PA Images/Alamy Stock Photo, p. 13 (bottom); Smith Archive/ Alamy Stock Photo, pp. 14, 19 (bottom); Alamy Stock Photo, p. 17 (top); ITAR-TASS/ Alamy Stock Photo, p. 17 (bottom); AP Photo/CTK, p. 18; Smith Archive/Alamy Stock Photo, p. 19 (top); AP Photo/Craig Fujii, p. 20; AP Photo/JOHN MCCONNICO, p. 21 (top); AP Photo/JOHN GAPS, p. 21 (bottom); AP Photo/Rebecca Blackwell, p. 24; AP Photo/Julie Jacobson, p. 25 (top); AP Photo/KYDPL KYODO, p. 25 (bottom); AP Photo/Kyodo Extra, p. 26; AP Photo/Yomiuri Shimbun, p. 27 (top); AP Photo/DPA (Photostream), p. 27 (bottom).

Cover: Aflo Co., Ltd./Alamy Stock photo; Eugene Onischenko/Shutterstock.com; Petr Toman/Shutterstock.com.